The Nicest Gift

E
C3

to the
Boys and Girls
of
East Los Angeles

n the outskirts of Los Angeles, in the neighborhood known as the Barrio, Carlitos lives with his father and mother. His dog Blanco lives there too. *Blanco* means "white," and Blanco is a white dog. But the house that Blanco and Carlitos and Carlitos' father and mother live in is a very bright pink.

The Barrio is quaint and picturesque. The brightly painted houses cling to the steep slopes of the hills, and narrow roads wind up and down the hillsides. Here and there you can see cactus plants and corn patches that look just like the countryside of Old Mexico, which is where Carlitos' mother and father came from. Far in the distance Carlitos can see the city's tall buildings.

Carlitos and Blanco often play in the front yard. They like to play *caballito*. *Caballito* means "little horse."

"Giddy up! Giddy up!" Carlitos calls as they trot around.

Blanco's dark eyes and nose glisten in the sunshine and look like three black buttons sewn onto his white coat. In the Barrio, the sun shines even in the winter.

Carlitos' mother likes plants and flowers. She never throws away old jars; instead, she keeps them to plant more flowers in, and then she places the pots and jars everywhere at the entrance to their house. There are even plants and flowers hanging from the tree branches in the yard. Mother also grows tomatoes, red peppers, and other spices to flavor her *tamales*.

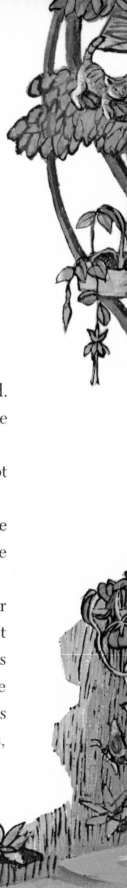

Inside, Carlitos and Blanco like to watch Mother cook *tamales*.

Tamales are made of corn meal, meat, and red chili peppers. They are wrapped in corn husks and cooked in a large kettle of boiling water.

Mother makes such good *tamales* that Carlitos and Blanco go around with their noses in the air, sniffing the good aroma that fills the house.

They can hardly wait for the *tamales* to be ready to eat.

At night, a stuffed Blanco sleeps at the foot of Carlitos' bed.

Sometimes, while Carlitos is sleeping Blanco crawls onto the bed, and then when Carlitos wakes up in the morning, he finds his dog curled up in his arms. Sometimes he even finds Blanco asleep on his head.

Carlitos loves his dog Blanco so much that he wouldn't know what to do without him.

ne of the things Carlitos and Blanco like to do best is to go with Mother to the *mercado* to buy groceries and other things for the house. The *mercado* is the marketplace. On their way, they greet good friends, because in the Barrio everyone knows everyone else.

"*Buenas días, Carlitos.*"

"Good morning, Carlitos."

There is much to see and do at the *mercado*, and always there is the *churro* wagon parked nearby. When smoke comes from the little chimney, Carlitos knows the *churro* man inside the wagon is cooking *churros*. *Churros* are made of sweet dough and cooked in a large kettle of boiling oil. When they are done, they look like huge pretzels.

Looking around, Carlitos sees a bunch of colored balloons dancing in the air just a short hop from the *churro* wagon, so he knows his friend Leandro is there too. Leandro is a jolly old man. He has on a large straw hat, and to attract attention to what he has to sell, he calls out his wares as if he were singing a song:

"*Balones!*"　　"Balloons!"

"*Cacahuatitos!*"　　"Peanuts!"

When he sees Carlitos, he calls out:

"*Come está, Carlitos?*"

"How are you, Carlitos?"

And Carlitos is pleased to answer:

"*Bien, Señor Leandro!*"

"Fine, Mister Leandro!"

Old Leandro likes Blanco too and always pats him on the head. "Blanco's head is as white as mine," the old man says.

25¢

CACAHUATITOS

10¢

Leandro sells his wares at the entrance to the *mercado*. Inside, the *mercado* is colorful and gay with restaurants and shops that sell all kinds of foods and Mexican merchandise. There is singing and dancing almost all of the time—but especially at Christmas time.

Of course Carlitos likes to stop at the toy shop. Here there are *piñatas* of all shapes and colors hanging overhead. There are puppets, *boleros*, spinning tops, and many other kinds of wooden toys. There is also a lot of confusion.

But even in the confusion, Carlitos can find what he likes best: the *payaso* wagon. *Payaso* means "clown." When he pulls the wagon, the clown does somersaults and other acrobatic stunts that make Blanco bark and run.

Carlitos is laughing at the little clown. Because he is busy tugging at his mother's skirt to ask her to come and see the clown, he fails to see Blanco run away. Poor Blanco has never seen a clown do somersaults before!

Poor Carlitos doesn't know what he will do without Blanco. He can't remember ever playing in the front yard without him before.

When Father returns from work in the evening, he goes with Carlitos to look for Blanco. They climb the steep slopes of the hills, and they walk on all the winding roads, and they look behind all the cactus plants, but there is no Blanco.

Heartbroken, Carlitos has to go to bed without his dog.

All day long, the next day, Carlitos wears himself out sitting on the front steps and calling Blanco. It is Christmas Eve, and to cheer him up, his mother surprises him with the clown wagon he liked so much at the *mercado*. But what good is the toy if his dog isn't there to play with it too?

eanwhile, Blanco has gone back to the *mercado* to look for Carlitos. His white fur is now gray with dust, and he is limping on one of his hind legs.

"Poor little dog," old Leandro is thinking. He doesn't know it is Blanco, because Blanco is white and this dog is gray. But before the old man can do something for him, the dog disappears between the legs of the crowd and hobbles out of sight.

From time to time Blanco will stop and look up to see if someone cares to help him find his way home, but everyone is talking and laughing, and shouting and singing, and saying, *"Feliz Navidad!"* And no one takes any notice of the little lost dusty gray dog.

Someone even steps on his paw.

Finally Blanco comes to a side street away from the noisy crowd and dangerous traffic.

Here, there is a little church with an open door.
The church is dark and almost deserted except for the
lighted Nativity scene at the end of the aisle.

As Blanco limps down the aisle, music is playing.

    "Noche de paz..."   "Night of peace..."

    "Noche de amor..."   "Night of love..."

Blanco is very weary by now. All he wants to do is sleep. Curling up on the floor of warm straw near the Christ-Child, he feels safe and peaceful for the first time since losing Carlitos.

He falls asleep in no time at all.

Christmas morning, Carlitos wakes up sad. There is still no Blanco in his bed, and he is sad when his mother says, *"Feliz Navidad"* and just as sad when his father says, *"Feliz Navidad."* He is still sad when all three of them go to the little church for Christmas Mass. (Because they should be four, you know.)

Taking their seats inside the church, Carlitos sees something stirring near the Nativity scene. "Look, Mama!" he cries. "There is a little gray dog that looks like Blanco."

He nudges his father. "See, Papa? The music must have wakened him. Doesn't he look just like Blanco?"

The little gray dog pricks up his ears.
You know why . . . he hears his name. He hears Carlitos' voice and comes
limping down the aisle faster and faster and leaps right into Carlitos' arms.

"Mama! Papa! It *is* Blanco," Carlitos cries.

At home after the Mass, Father fixes Blanco's sore leg and puts a bandage on it, while Mother cooks her very best Christmas dinner. *Tamales* and *churros*!

And after supper, Carlitos and Blanco play with the toy wagon. While Carlitos pulls the wagon, Blanco barks at the clown. But this time he doesn't run away. After all, a toy clown is just a toy. Like his rubber bone! Nothing to be afraid of.

Carlitos also knows that a toy clown is just a toy. It's fun to play with the clown—that's true—but what really makes him happy is having Blanco home again. It is the nicest Christmas gift he could ever have wished for.